the VERY WORST ever

FLUSHED AWAY WATER PARK

BY ANDY NONAMUS
ILLUSTRATED BY AMY JINDRA

LITTLE SIMON
NEW YORK   AMSTERDAM/ANTWERP   LONDON
TORONTO   SYDNEY/MELBOURNE   NEW DELHI

This book is a work of fiction. Any references to historical events, real people, or real places are used fictitiously. Other names, characters, places, and events are products of the author's imagination, and any resemblance to actual events or places or persons, living or dead, is entirely coincidental.

LITTLE SIMON
An imprint of Simon & Schuster Children's Publishing Division
1230 Avenue of the Americas, New York, New York 10020
First Little Simon hardcover edition May 2025
© 2025 by Simon & Schuster, LLC
Also available in a Little Simon paperback edition.
All rights reserved, including the right of reproduction in whole or in part in any form.
LITTLE SIMON is a registered trademark of Simon & Schuster, LLC, and associated colophon is a trademark of Simon & Schuster, LLC.
For information about special discounts for bulk purchases, please contact Simon & Schuster Special Sales at 1-866-506-1949 or business@simonandschuster.com.
The Simon & Schuster Speakers Bureau can bring authors to your live event. For more information or to book an event contact the Simon & Schuster Speakers Bureau at 1-866-248-3049 or visit our website at www.simonspeakers.com.
Book design by Hannah Frece
The illustrations for this book were rendered digitally.
The text of this book was set in Causten Round.
Manufactured in the United States of America 0425 LAK
10 9 8 7 6 5 4 3 2 1
CIP data for this book is available from the Library of Congress.
ISBN 9781665973540 (hc)
ISBN 9781665973533 (pbk)
ISBN 9781665973557 (ebook)

CONTENTS

	INTRODUCTION LETTER	
CHAPTER 1	SCHOOL DAY, P. P. POOL DAY	1
CHAPTER 2	MAYBE MERMAIDS	13
CHAPTER 3	MOMMY'S WITTLE BABY	31
CHAPTER 4	NEIGH	45
CHAPTER 5	THE LUNCH POOL	59
CHAPTER 6	LET'S GET FLUSHED!	73
CHAPTER 7	OFF THE FLOAT	85
CHAPTER 8	THE SANDCASTLE LIFE	93
CHAPTER 9	SLIP-SLIDING TO DOOM	103
CHAPTER 10	LAST SPLASH	113

Hey, Reader!

Thanks for checking out my story. Though I gotta warn you, I can't ever let you know my real name or what I look like. This may seem weird, but trust me, it's very important that I stay a secret.

Why? To protect myself! Seriously, these stories are super embarrassing!

Plus, you might even know me already! I could be in your class, on your ping-pong team, in your dance club, or bringing burned cupcakes to your bake sale . . . anywhere!

Hi!

For all you know I could be sitting next to you right now!

So I went ahead and scratched out my name and put a sticker on my face, so you don't have to. You're welcome.

Now, we can both enjoy reading all about my awkward life . . . if you're into that kind of thing.

Peace out!

1

SCHOOL DAY, P. P. POOL DAY

Have you ever wondered what makes a school bus full of kids smoosh their faces against the window like fish in a way-too-crowded fish tank?

Well, here is the answer: a field trip to the water park.

"LOOK!" I cackled into the glass. "WE'RE HERE. WE'RE FINALLY HERE."

Hey—I'm just like any other kid. There's no need to play it cool when it's field-trip day.

I peeled my face off the window and bounced in my cracked, old, sticky bus seat with purple goo oozing out of it.

I didn't care what that goo was. I didn't even care why one of my best pals, Jake Gold, was smelling it.

See, this field trip was special. Why? Because we were going to a *pool* instead of to *school*. And what do you learn in a pool? NOTHING! I don't even think studying is allowed in pools!

All you do is float and chill. And you can bet that I was ready for that.

As soon as the school bus door opened, we all spilled out.

A magical sign with a waving mermaid welcomed us. It read:

WELCOME TO
P. P. POOLS
THE NUMBER-ONE
WATER PARK
ADVENTURE
(SERIOUSLY.)

And beyond the sign was a world of waterslides, pools, and a lazy river that was *so* lazy, it helped even the most worried kids mellow out and go with the flow.

"Are you ready to shred some awesome waves in there?" asked Jake.

By "shred," Jake meant hop on a surfboard in the tidal wave pool.

By "awesome," Jake meant fun for him and too scary for me. Because I am not like Jake. Hmm, come to think of it, maybe no one is like Jake.

See, Jake loves sports and thinks that everyone else in the world loves sports as much as he does. And don't get me wrong. I like sports. But Jake loves sports the way I love candy . . . which, as my mom likes to say, is *too much.*

So while Jake was ready to rip it up, I was ready to float it down . . . in the lazy river.

But still I replied, "Yeah, sure."

Then an odd sight stepped in front of us.

It was Mr. Hughes, our teacher. He was wearing what he called a very special outfit for today.

It was a scuba suit with a mermaid-tail floatie wrapped around his belly.

Normally, this would be weird, but in my world... weird is very normal.

"Greetings, my school of fishy fishies!" Mr. Hughes called out. "Who is ready for an excellent day at the wet and wild P. P. Pools?"

Oh, he didn't have to ask twice.

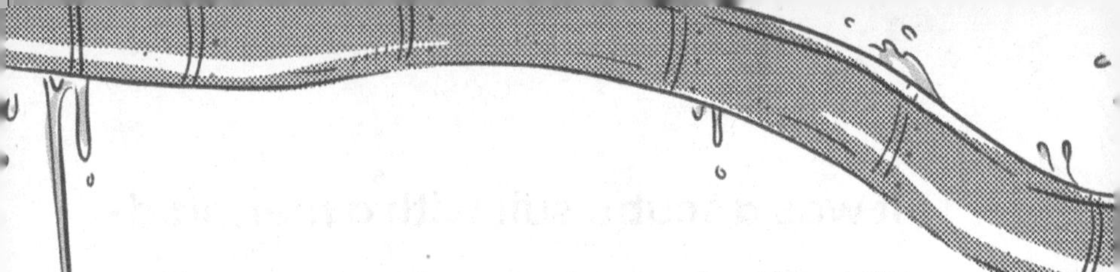

Every student started chanting: "P. P. Pools! P. P. Pools! P. P. Pools!"

"*Fin*-tastic!" said Mr. Hughes. "Please swim carefully this way as we get our tickets and dip our toes into excitement."

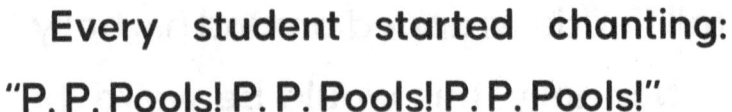

As I followed the others, I heard the sound of screams above me. I looked up to see the loops, drops, and monster-splash plops from kids on the waterslides that stretched high into the air.

Gulp.

I didn't even want to dip my pinky toe down one of those rides.

WATCH OUT FOR FALLING WATER

MAYBE MERMAIDS

"Don't worry, ▅▅▅▅▅▅▅. Those are screams of joy."

I knew that voice. It was Glinda Alegre, one of my best friends. She was dressed in black with a skull-and-crossbones barrette in her hair.

She was also one of the weirdest kids I had ever met.

"How can you tell those are happy screams?" I asked.

"Trust me," Glinda said. "You'll know when you hear a real danger scream."

Would I? I wanted to ask her how, but Jake had other ideas.

"We need a game plan, team," he said. "P. P. Pools is huge. There are at least fifty different water rides, and we need to catch them all."

"It's more like *a hundred* rides if you count the pools," said Regina du Lar as she walked up to us with a tablet in her hand. "So that's twice the fun!"

Regina was my other best friend. She was the brains of our group, which made Jake the muscle and Glinda . . . um, the darkness?

"Twice the fun? Sounds terrible. Count me out," said Glinda.

See what I mean?

"Hmm, okay. If we swim as fast as we can down every waterslide, then maybe we can make it," said Jake.

"Swimming down super-steep and slippery slides sounds really scary," I said.

"Did someone say *scary*?" asked Glinda. "Now I'm back in."

Again, see what I mean?

"There's no need to rush," said Regina. "I made a perfect plan last night on my computer. This program will tell us where the short lines are, so we can ride every ride!"

She held up her tablet, and what I saw looked like a mess of lines. But if Regina said the plan would work, it was going to work.

Especially if I found a way to skip the scary rides.

The second we stepped through the gates, my eyes sparkled and my jaw dropped.

Now do you see why this place was such a big deal? There were so many different pools and slides, I didn't know where to look first. Beach balls bounced around, kids sprang from diving boards, and there were more palm trees than I could count.

And then, I saw it. The Flushed Away waterslide. Kids called it the Hold-On-to-Your-Swim-Trunks Twister. It had loops, it had hoops, and I'm pretty sure I could see sliders flying through the air at one point of the ride. Oh, it was also shaped like a giant toilet.

Note to self: skip this ride at all costs.

"Good day, fellow adventurers!" said a man wearing a soaking-wet business suit. "I am Peter Peterson, owner of P. P. Pools. Welcome to my water world. We have pools with puppies, pools for dancing, and even a pool filled with ice cream. Now go have fun and . . . wait a moment."

He suddenly stopped speaking, then looked from side to side.

"Do you hear that splashing sound?" he asked.

Of course we heard splashing sounds. This was a water park full of kids, after all!

I shrugged and said, "The only thing *I* hear is the lazy river calling my name."

"No. It's *them* . . . *the mermaids*," Peter Peterson whispered. "They are making fun of my human toes!"

Then he pointed down at his very big and VERY hairy feet.

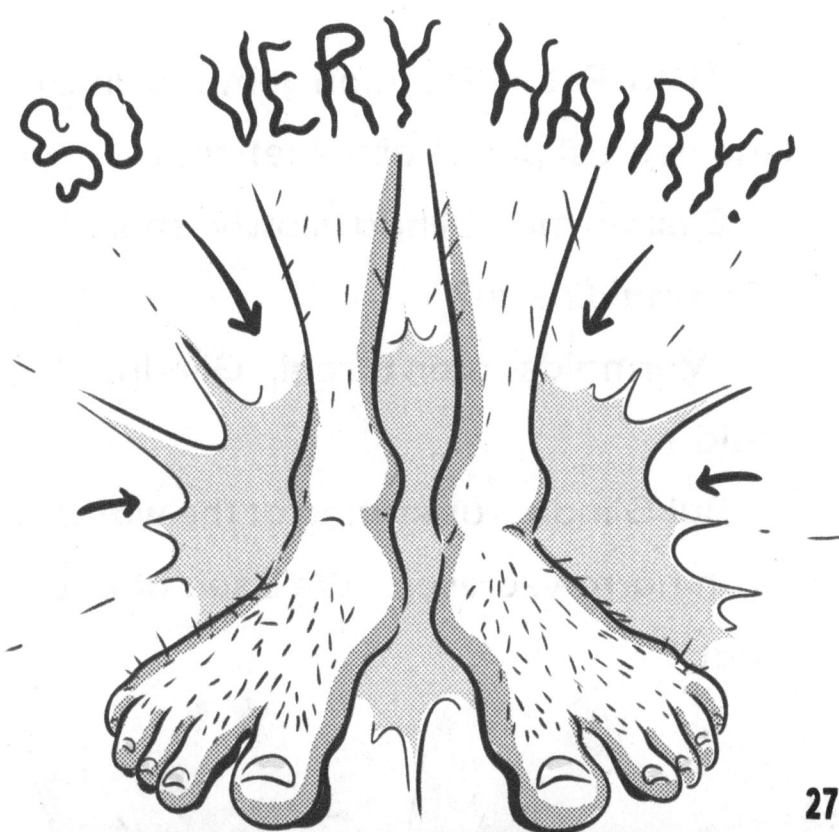

"We can't *all* have fish tails! Do you hear me, mermaids?" Peter Peterson shouted. "But that's a story for another time. Enjoy yourselves, friends. And if you see any mermaids, tell me right away."

Then Peter Peterson jumped into the nearest pool, hairy-feet-first.

Beside me, Glinda slowly smiled. "Mermaids, huh?"

"Mermaids aren't real, Glinda," I said.

But Glinda was staring at the water with narrowed eyes. "We'll see about that."

3
MOMMY'S WITTLE BABY

My friends and I hurried to the first waterslide. There was a line of kids heading up the steps to reach the top. The stairs stretched so high that I couldn't see where they ended.

Here's the thing about water parks: the rides last a few seconds, but the lines last forever.

But that gave us a chance to see exactly what kind of slide we were heading up to ride.

This one was a little-kid slide. How did I know? Duh, look at all the little kids in line ahead of us. Yep, this one was totally my speed.

"Hold on to your shorts, everyone!" I cheered as I reached the front of the line.

Just as I placed my foot on the first step, a hand reached out to block me.

"Don't forget your swimmy float," said a lady wearing a large sun hat.

Then she handed me a float with angel wings and a top part that said MOMMY'S WITTLE BABY.

"Um, no thanks," I said.

"Um, yes, thanks," she said. "You can't go down the slide without the float. And now you are holding up the line."

I turned around to see everyone in line giving me the evil eye ... even my friends!

"Just take the float and go," said Jake. "No one will see you."

What could I do? I took the float and went down the slide. And you know what? It was great!

Until I splashed into the pool at the bottom. Because I didn't just make a splash ... there was also a *flash*.

What happened next was the stuff of legends. Like, the bad kind of legends.

It started with a giggle, then it turned into a wave of laughter. But no one in the pool was looking at me. Nope, they were looking at the giant screens that were all over the park.

So I looked too. But I wish I didn't.

The screen had a giant picture of me going down the slide on this very silly float. But that's not the worst part.

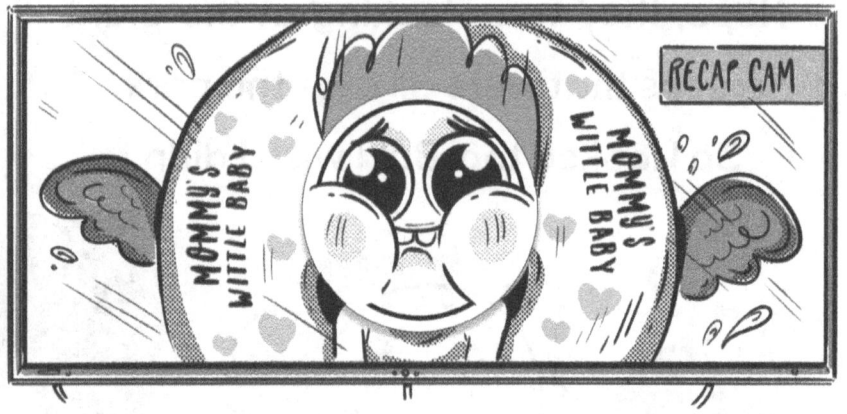

See, when I get scared on a ride, sometimes I make a face. It's not like an "I'm scared" face. It's more like an adorable baby face, the kind that makes aunts and grandmas want to squeeze those chubby little cheeks.

And now that face was on the big screen along with that no-good float. I was ready to sink to the bottom of the pool when Jake came to my rescue with a giant splash.

"LOOK OUT! DRAGON COMING THROUGH!" he screamed.

And it was true! He was riding the COOLEST-looking dragon float!

Then Regina came down on a DINOSAUR float!

"Aww, how come you got those great floats and I'm stuck with this baby one?" I asked.

"It's the power of the line," said Regina. "You get what you get."

Hmm, maybe that meant Glinda would get stuck with something silly and then the whole water park would forget about me on MOMMY'S WITTLE BABY.

Nope. Glinda glided down the slide softly on a unicorn float . . . and she made it look so cool!

"Next! Next! What ride is next?" Jake cheered. "There are so many choices I just can't decide. Ah! Jake … brain … ouch!"

"Relax. We've got Regina's map," I told my friend.

"Well, I can't bring a tablet in the pool," Regina said. "But I do have my waterproof phone."

Regina pulled her phone out, tapped the screen, and a small laser projected a map into the air.

A robotic voice spoke from the phone. "Next stop: the Wild, Wild Waves for cowboy surfboarding."

"YEEHAW!" Jake shouted. "Let's ride!"

4

NEIGH

Here's one thing I know: Mommy's Wittle Baby would never get on a surfboard in a pool called the Wild, Wild Waves.

Maybe that's why I said, "Yes, let's ride those waves and I'll go first."

I looked around for any cameras while we were in line.

If I was going to be up on the big screen again, I needed to look really cool.

One *wittle* problem: I am not always the "really cool" type of kid.

Want proof? When we reached the front of the line, a park worker gave me a rocking-horse surfboard and a cowboy hat.

"What's this?" I asked.

"It's for the ride," he explained. "Everyone needs to use them. Except for the girl with the unicorn float. That thing is awesome!"

"I know," said Glinda.

So I put on my hat and looked at the horse board.

"Does this look cool?" I asked.

"Neigh," the horse board said back.

"Let's hit the water," said Jake as he pushed us all in.

The wild waves were easy at first, but then they started getting wilder.

Everyone else was having a blast, but I was holding on for dear life.

Jake swerved by me and said, "YEEHAW, PARTNER! ARE YOU HAVING A BLAST?"

"NEIGH!" my horse board called out. "NEIGH!"

"Don't listen to my horse board!" I said. "I am having so much fun! Can't you tell?"

"Neigh," my horse board huffed again.

Regina surfed up next.

"Okay, everyone!" she said. "They are about to shift to bucking-bronco waves, so don't let go!"

"What happens if we let go?" I asked.

"The mermaids will get us," said someone.

I turned and saw Glinda floating by on her unicorn like the waves were not even there.

"Ha ha," I said. "Very funny."

But Glinda didn't smile. Instead, she said, "Here come the big waves."

And she was right. *BOOM!* It was like I was trapped in a storm at sea! The whole world sloshed around me.

Regina was thrown first. She flew into the air but had time to take the perfect selfie before making the perfect splash.

"My turn!" said Jake as he jumped off his horse and made an even bigger splash.

But me, I was going to hold on until the end! I leaned back on my horse board and smiled for all the cameras to see.

"Look at me! I'm king cowboy of the wild, wild waves!" I shouted.

But my horse board said, "Neigh."

And my horse board was right. I guess kings can't surf either, because the next wild wave flipped me over and I bounced right off Glinda's unicorn float.

It was like getting double-bounced on a trampoline on the moon. I flew up so high, I could see the whole water park. And the whole water park could see me, too.

The worst part about going up is that you have to come down. And boy did I ever come down with a crushing splash in the pool.

But when I came up, people weren't laughing at me anymore. They were cheering! I'd done it!

I just wished my swim trunks hadn't floated up beside me one minute later.

5

THE LUNCH POOL

Did I tell you that P. P. Pools feels like it's never-ending?

I had no idea one place could have so many different pools.

We swam in the Slime Pool. Well, at least, we tried. You couldn't really swim in it. You just kinda sunk in it, then slipped around.

We swam in the Puppy Pool. It was filled with puppies and water . . . so it had that perfect wet dog smell. Yeah, it was gross and cute at the same time.

The Frozen Arctic Pool was fun too . . . if you liked floating around inside a giant ice cube.

But when Regina's map sent us to the Swamp Pool, my stomach made a noise. It was somewhere between a gurgle and a lion's roar. It was so loud that the frogs ribbitted back at me.

Regina laughed. "Sounds like you're ready for the Lunch Pool."

Glinda floated by on her unicorn in the murky green water.

"The mermaids don't want to hear your stomach anymore," she said. "Let's go eat."

So we went to the Lunch Pool.

Okay, I know what you're wondering. Is it gross to swim in a pool that has food floating everywhere? *Nope!* It's the best!

Regina ordered an ice-cream cone from a floating cart, Glinda grabbed snacks for the "mermaids," and Jake was eating a submarine sandwich.

Me? I swam in zigzags, leaving my mouth open so that all sorts of treats could float right in.

I was about to eat a churro when I realized that it wasn't a churro at all. It was the top of a snorkel.

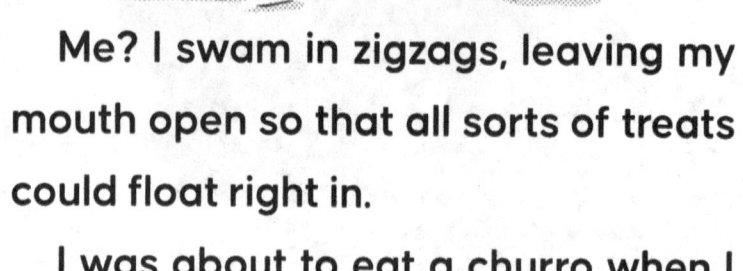

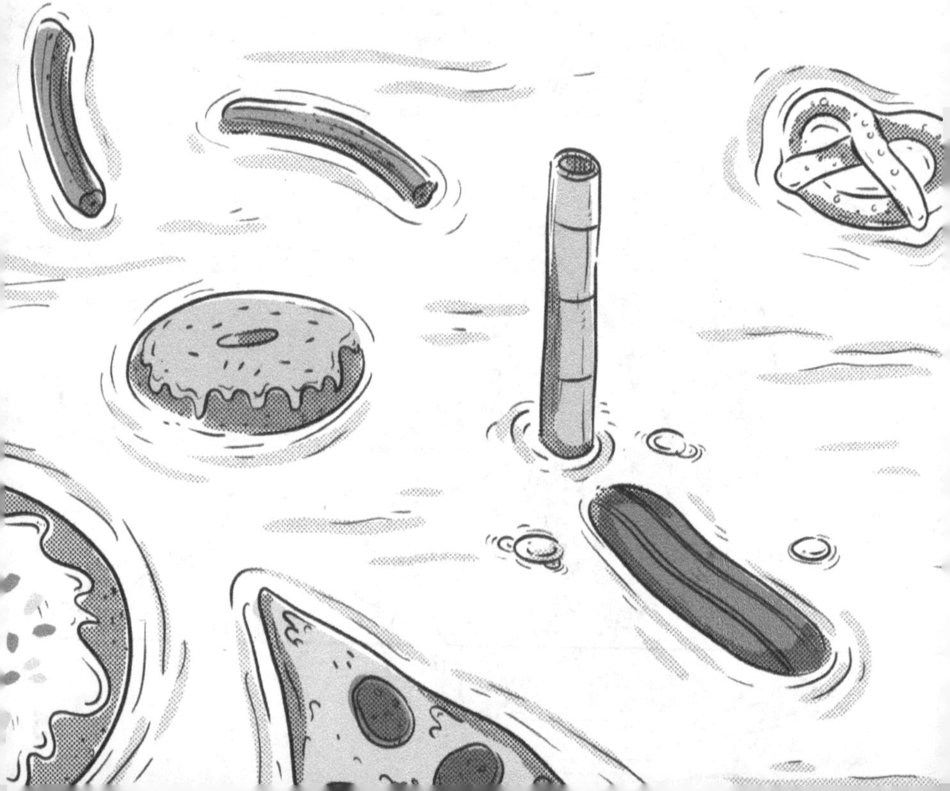

"AHH!" I shouted.

Peter Peterson popped out of the pool and pointed at me.

"Where am I?" he asked. "You are not a mermaid...are you?"

"You're in the Lunch Pool," I said. "And I am not a mermaid."

"Hmm, but I've seen you somewhere before," he said. "Ah yes! *Mommy's Wittle Baby!* Hahaha! That must have been very embarrassing for you."

What do you say to that? I decided to eat a cookie that floated by.

But Peter Peterson grabbed the cookie out of my hand and said, "Ah, drat! I was chasing a mermaid and must have taken a wrong turn. Best to get a snack before I set out again."

Then he stuffed the soggy sweet into the top of his snorkel, slurped it down, and swam away.

"Watch out for the mermaids," he warned. "Oh, and stay far from the Flushed Away ride. It's much too daring for a *wittle baby* like you."

Wait, did the guy searching for mermaids just make fun of me?

6

LET'S GET FLUSHED!

Can you guess what ride was next ride on Regina's magic map?

Yep. It was Flushed Away. You remember? The ride that looks like a giant toilet.

Normally I would say, *Gross, no thank you, I'm not ever going on that ride.* But today wasn't normal.

I wasn't going to let Peter Peterson the mermaid hunter be right. I was nobody's *wittle baby*.

Okay, I guess my mom said I would always be her little baby . . . but that was back in the real world. And this wasn't the real world.

This was P. P. Pools water park.

Lucky for me, the ride had a very long line. It rose up and up and up into the distance. We were going to be here for hours.

I gave a little whisper-cheer to myself. "Yay, line."

"Oh, are you worried about the line?" asked Glinda. "I can get us up there in no time."

I didn't like the sound of that. Not one bit.

"No, we should wait," I said. "It's the fair thing to do."

Then we saw a sign that told us how long we'd have to wait in line from this point. All it said was: FOREVER.

"Aww, *forever*?" cried Jake. "I can't wait that long. Let's do Glinda's plan."

I cannot describe the look on Glinda's face. It was the sort of happy evil that only villains get. Then she put her plan into action.

"Hey, everyone!" Glinda called out. "Make way for MOMMY'S WITTLE BABY!"

The crowd gasped and turned to stare at me. I started to panic. And here's the thing: when I get panicked, I get the same face as when I'm scared.

Yep, my cute baby face was back.

The crowd gasped and started cheering, "WITTLE BABY! WITTLE BABY!"

I was ready to hide, but that wasn't part of Glinda's plan. She had Jake put us all onto her unicorn float, and the kids in line surfed us all the way from the end of the line to the front.

A park worker in surfer clothes stood by the slide entrance.

"Yo! What's up, Wittle Baby and friends?" he said. "This is Flushed Away! Don't worry, this ride is super fun. Just hop on the giant float and get flushed."

He pointed over to a round float that could hold all four of us. It looked soft. It looked cozy. It looked safe.

Hey, maybe this ride was going to be just fine.

So we climbed onto the float, and that's when the worker said, "Cool. Just remember to stay on the float at all times."

"What happens if we don't?" I asked.

"I have no idea," said the worker. "It's what my boss told me I had to start saying ... after that one time."

"WHAT ONE TIME?!" I cried.

"It's not important, Wittle Baby," the worker said. "Just hold on, have fun, and make that adorable face again!"

"WAIT! WAIT!" I screamed.

But the worker said, "I heard GREAT, GREAT! Now let's get FLUSHED!"

Then he jumped up and pulled down on a giant toilet handle to start the ride.

7

OFF THE FLOAT

"WAHHHHHHHHHHHHHHHHHHHHHHHHHHHHHHHHHHHHH!"

That scream you heard? It was us as we whipped around and around the bowl.

Have you ever been flushed down a toilet? Well, let me tell you: it's not that much fun.

The water underneath us rushed fast as we swirled closer and closer to the hole at the bottom.

Random splashes shot out at us from all sides. I really hoped they didn't use real toilet water for this ride.

Blech.

Finally, we reached the dark hole and I stopped screaming . . . because our float slowed to a stop.

Was that it? Oh, wow! I'd made it! Wittle Baby had survived the very scary ride! Flushed Away was over!

Except it wasn't.

A new clicking sound came from underneath us. Then our float started going up a glass tube like a roller coaster.

Once again, I could see the whole park beneath us. All the pools, all the swimmers, and the tops of the palm trees.

I pointed down and laughed. "Look— there's Mr. Hughes!"

Our teacher was in a pool filled with floaties, and he was totally asleep. We could hear him snoring from a mile away. Because we were probably a mile up in the air!

"Careful, Wittle Baby," said Glinda. "If you keep smiling, everyone will think you're having a good time."

Whoa. Glinda was right! I *was* having a good time.

Until we reached the top of the tunnel. That's when we hit a straight-down drop!

Our float spun round and round in circles as it fell onto another ramp that launched us up into the air again.

For a moment, we were all there together, frozen midflight.

Jake's hair looked perfect.

Regina took another great selfie.

Even Glinda's unicorn somehow came back to find her.

And me? I was falling off the float.

8
THE SANDCASTLE LIFE

I watched as my friends and my float floated away from me. I tried to swim back to everyone, but the ride had other ideas.

It flushed me into a smaller tunnel that was filled with water sprayers. As I slid around, I was hit with water from every direction.

I felt like a car going through a car wash. At least I would be squeaky clean when this was all over.

But then the tunnel launched me to the last place I expected ... onto dry land.

It felt like a sandy beach, but I couldn't see anything.

The world around me was pitch-black except for a tiny light in the distance.

"Hello?" I called out.

"Hello?" my voice echoed back to me.

Yeah. It was super CREEPY!

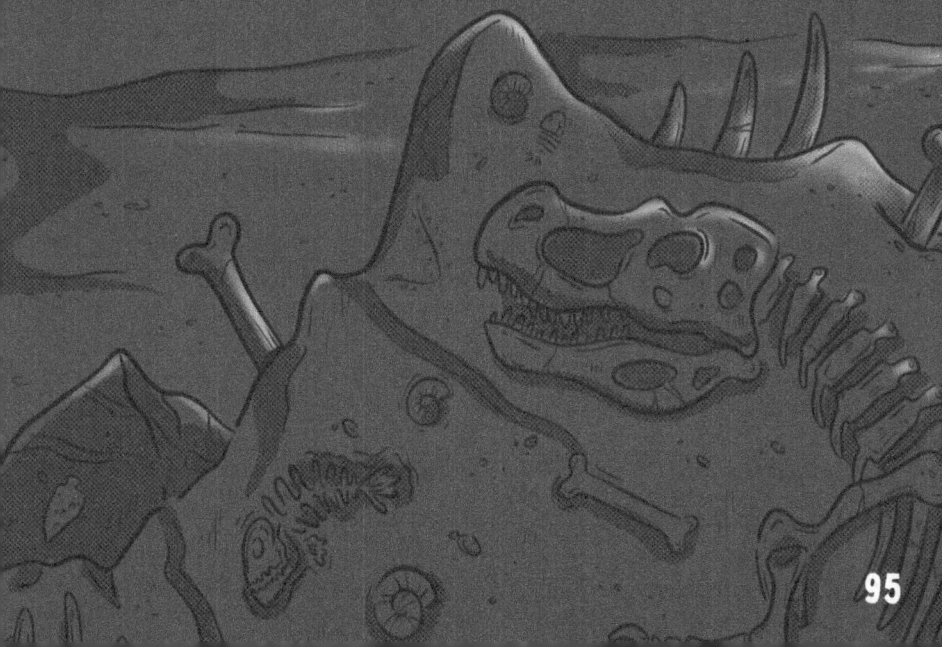

"Um . . . is anyone there? Peter Peterson?" I called out. "Mermaids?"

This time no one answered. Not even my echo. And yes, that was WAY SUPER CREEPIER!

As I sat in the sand, a lot of thoughts popped into my head.

Was this it? Was this where I lived from now on? Would I need to build a sandcastle house and learn to fish for loose candy that fell out of kids' pockets on the Flushed Away ride?

I pictured my life sleeping on a bed of sand, and I knew it wasn't for me. Even if the free candy sounded good.

I needed to get home to my mom and my friends and my weird school that took field trips to water parks! I needed to escape!

There was just one way out of this darkness. Toward the tiny light. And I was not scared. Not at all! Because I'm not a wittle baby.

Oh, who am I kidding? I was totally freaked out. But you know what? Even not-wittle-babies can be *totally* freaked out.

So I ran to the light and heard a splashing sound.

It was water! And water leads back to the water park! Or the ocean. Or a sewer. Whatever. It would lead me somewhere that wasn't here!

As I ran, the splashing got louder and louder. The sand under my feet got wetter and wetter. Which was a problem.

Because do you know another word for wet sand? *Mud.*

And do you know what mud is? *Slippery.*

So it wasn't long before I stopped running and started slipping and sliding to my doom.

9

SLIP-SLIDING TO DOOM

Why was I heading to my doom? Oh, because guess what was hiding at the end of the darkness in that tiny bit of light.

A waterfall.

How was there a hidden waterfall on this ride? I don't know. I was just going with the flow.

As I watched the waterfall ahead, I had an odd feeling wash over me. It was a feeling that I should treat this ride like a lazy river and just relax. So I lay back and closed my eyes. I pretended it was a good time.

Then a new float appeared that looked like a mermaid's tail. It just popped up from nowhere and cradled me, so I went with it.

Me, the mermaid-tail float, and the waterfall. We were meant to be together.

As we flew over the waterfall, it wasn't scary. In fact, it was almost like I was in a dream. My float and I, we didn't crash. We drifted down the waterfall and followed where the water went.

Right into the lazy river!

All around me were other kids asleep on their floats. We drifted down the lazy river without a care in the world.

One kid turned to me and said, "Hey, you're Mommy's Wittle Baby."

And I said, "Yep. I am."

It didn't bother me anymore! I was in a state of pure joy.

I didn't even notice when my float stopped. Other kids floated by, but I just stayed there. Then I looked and saw that I was right next to the end of the Flushed Away ride.

I hopped out to meet up with my friends, but then I saw the mermaid-tail float wave goodbye.

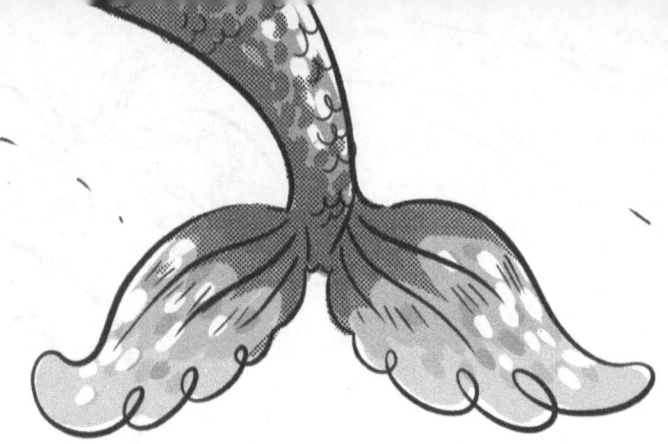

"Thanks so much!" I called out. "But... what are you?!"

The mermaid-tail float did not answer. Instead, it threw a paper airplane toward me.

I caught it and saw there was writing on it. It was a note!

I unfolded the paper airplane to read:

> PLEASE TELL THE HAIRY-FOOTED MAN TO STOP LOOKING FOR US! WE DON'T LIKE HUMAN FEET!

Huh?

When I looked back, the mermaid-tail float was gone.

Like I told you before, weird is my normal. So I shrugged and went to find my friends.

10

LAST SPLASH

Regina was the first to hug me.

"We were so worried about you!" she said.

Then Jake gave us both a giant bear hug.

"Dude, you totally broke the one rule of the ride," Jake said. "Are you okay?"

And Glinda?

She didn't look worried about me at all. Or maybe she looked a little worried that I was okay. Hmm. She's hard to read sometimes.

"I'm good," I said. "But I am done water-parking."

Mr. Hughes must have heard me. Because he waddled over and said, "Okay, students! Our swim time is done—please make your way out of the pools and onto dry land!"

Everyone groaned and complained as we left the pool. But me? I had a job to do.

I searched the crowd for Peter Peterson and found him by the gift shop. He was easy to spot in his very wet business suit.

"Excuse me," I said. "I think this is meant for you."

I handed over the paper airplane.

"Hmm," Peter Peterson said. "A paper airplane at a water park isn't the best gift. It's paper ... and water is the natural enemy of paper! Next time you should give me something better. But not from our gift shop. I already have everything we sell."

"It's also a note," I pointed out.

Peter Peterson unfolded the paper and his mouth dropped open. "You've done it. You've found them . . . the mermaids."

Then he did a dance and squished the note against his soaking-wet jacket.

"Your secret is safe with me," he whispered to the note as he put it away.

Did the water park have mermaids? Did they save me from a wild toilet bowl ride? I may never know.

But I did know that I had a splash with my friends. And I even had a picture to prove it.